Bill Martin Jr

Polar Bear, Polar Bear, What Do You Hear?

Illustrated by Eric Carle

PUFFIN BOOKS

Polar Bear, Polar Bear,
what do you hear?

I hear a lion
roaring in my ear.

Lion, Lion,
what do you hear?

I hear a hippopotamus
snorting in my ear.

Hippopotamus, Hippopotamus,
what do you hear?

I hear a flamingo
fluting in my ear.

Zebra, Zebra,
what do you hear?

I hear a boa constrictor
hissing in my ear.

Boa Constrictor, Boa Constrictor,
what do you hear?

I hear an elephant
trumpeting in my ear.

Elephant, Elephant,
what do you hear?

I hear a leopard
snarling in my ear.

Leopard, Leopard,
what do you hear?

I hear a peacock
yelping in my ear.

Peacock, Peacock,
what do you hear?

I hear a walrus
bellowing in my ear.

Walrus, Walrus,
what do you hear?

I hear a zookeeper
whistling in my ear.

Zookeeper, Zookeeper,
what do you hear?

I hear children . . .

. . . growling like a polar bear,
roaring like a lion,
snorting like a hippopotamus,
fluting like a flamingo,
braying like a zebra,
hissing like a boa constrictor,
trumpeting like an elephant,
snarling like a leopard,
yelping like a peacock,
bellowing like a walrus . . .

that's what I hear.

Some other Puffin picture books by Bill Martin Jr with Eric Carle

BROWN BEAR, BROWN BEAR, WHAT DO YOU SEE?

Some other Puffin picture books by Eric Carle

1, 2, 3 TO THE ZOO
THE BAD-TEMPERED LADYBIRD
DO YOU WANT TO BE MY FRIEND?
DRAW ME A STAR
FROM HEAD TO TOE
LITTLE CLOUD
THE MIXED-UP CHAMELEON
ROOSTER'S OFF TO SEE THE WORLD
THE TINY SEED
TODAY IS MONDAY
THE VERY HUNGRY CATERPILLAR

PUFFIN BOOKS

Published by the Penguin Group
Penguin Books Ltd, 80 Strand, London WC2R 0RL, England
Penguin Putnam Inc., 375 Hudson Street, New York, New York 10014, USA
Penguin Books Australia Ltd, 250 Camberwell Road, Camberwell, Victoria 3124, Australia
Penguin Books Canada Ltd, 10 Alcorn Avenue, Toronto, Ontario, Canada M4V 3B2
Penguin Books India (P) Ltd, 11 Community Centre, Panchsheel Park, New Delhi – 110 017, India
Penguin Books (NZ) Ltd, Cnr Rosedale and Airborne Roads, Albany, Auckland, New Zealand
Penguin Books (South Africa) (Pty) Ltd, 24 Sturdee Avenue, Rosebank 2196, South Africa

Penguin Books Ltd, Registered Offices: 80 Strand, London WC2R 0RL, England

www.penguin.com

First published in the United States by Henry Holt and Company, Inc 1991
First published in Great Britain by Hamish Hamilton Ltd 1992
Published in Picture Puffins 1994
20 19

Text copyright © Bill Martin Jr, 1991
Illustrations copyright © Eric Carle, 1991
All rights reserved

The moral right of the author and illustrator has been asserted

Manufactured in China by Imago

British Library Cataloguing in Publication Data
A CIP catalogue record for this book is available from the British Library

0–140–54519–0